THIS WALKER BOOK BELONGS TO:

_____

_____

_____

_____

ACKNOWLEDGEMENTS

Each story in this collection has been previously
published by Walker Books; each as a self-contained
volume, except "The Three Billy-goats Gruff" which was
taken from *The Three Little Pigs and Other Favourite
Nursery Stories* illustrated by Charlotte Voake, and
"Miss Polly" which was taken from *Stamp Your Feet,*
action rhymes chosen by Sarah Hayes, illustrated by
Toni Goffe.

First published 1997 by
Walker Books Ltd
87 Vauxhall Walk, London SE11 5H

This edition published 2000

10 9 8 7 6 5 4 3 2

Printed in Hong Kong

British Library Cataloguing in Publication Data
A catalogue record for this book is available from
the British Library.

ISBN 0-7445-7796-9

WALKER BOOKS
AND SUBSIDIARIES
LONDON • BOSTON • SYDNEY

THE WALKER TREASURY OF
FIRST
STORIES

30
PICTURE BOOK
FAVOURITES

Contents

In the Rain
with
Baby Duck

Pit-pat.
Pit-a-pat.
Pit-a-pit-a-pat.
Oh, the rain came down. It poured and poured. Baby Duck was cross. She did not like walking in the rain. But it was Pancake Sunday, a Duck family tradition, and Baby loved pancakes.

And she loved Grandpa, who was waiting on the other side of town.

Pit-pat. Pit-a-pat. Pit-a-pit-a-pat.

"Follow us! Step lively!" Mr and Mrs Duck left the house arm in arm.

"Wet feet," wailed Baby.

"Don't dally, dear. Don't drag behind," called Mr Duck.

by **Amy Hest**
illustrated by **Jill Barton**

"Wet face," pouted Baby. "Water in my eyes."

Mrs Duck pranced along. "See how the rain rolls off your back!"

"Mud," muttered Baby. "Mud, mud, mud."

"Don't dawdle, dear! Don't lag behind!"

Mr and Mrs Duck skipped ahead. They waddled. They shimmied. They hopped in all the puddles. Baby dawdled. She dallied and pouted and dragged behind.

She sang a little song.

I do not like the rain one bit
Splashing down my neck.
Baby feathers soaking wet,
I do not like this mean old day."

"Are you singing?" called Mr and Mrs Duck. "What a fine thing to do in the rain!"

Baby stopped singing.

Grandpa was waiting at the front door. He put his arm round Baby.

"Wet feet?" he asked.

"Yes," Baby said.

"Wet face?" Grandpa asked.

"Yes," Baby said.

"Mud?" Grandpa asked.

"Yes," Baby said. "Mud, mud, mud."

"I'm afraid the rain makes Baby cranky," clucked Mr Duck.

"I've never heard of a duck who doesn't like rain," worried Mrs Duck.

"Oh, really?" Grandpa kissed Baby's cheeks.

Grandpa took Baby's hand.

"Come with me, Baby."

They went upstairs to the attic.

"We are looking for a tall, green bag," Grandpa said.

Finally they found it. Inside was a beautiful red umbrella. There were matching boots, too.

"These used to be your mother's," Grandpa whispered. "A long time ago, she was a baby duck who did not like rain."

Baby opened the umbrella. The boots were just the right size.

Baby and Grandpa marched downstairs.

"My boots!" cried Mrs Duck. "And my bunny umbrella!"

"No, mine!" said Baby.

"You look lovely," said Mrs Duck.

Mr Duck put a plate of pancakes on the table. After that, Baby and Grandpa went outside.

Pit-pat. Pit-a-pat. Pit-a-pit-a-pat.

Oh, the rain came down. It poured and poured. Baby Duck and Grandpa walked arm in arm in the rain.

They waddled.

They shimmied.

They hopped in all the puddles.

And Baby Duck sang a new song.

"I really like the rain a lot
*   Splashing my umbrella.*
Big red boots on baby feet,
*   I really love this rainy day."*

The Three
Billy Goats Gruff

illustrated by
Charlotte Voake

Once upon a time three billy-goats lived together in a field on a hillside. Their names were Big Billy-goat Gruff, Middle Billy-goat Gruff, and Little Billy-goat Gruff.

A river ran beside the billy-goats' field, and one day they decided to cross it, to eat the grass on the other side. But first they had to go over the bridge, and under the bridge lived a great ugly Troll.

First Little Billy-goat Gruff stepped on to the bridge.

TRIP TRAP, TRIP TRAP, went his hoofs.

"Who's that tripping over my bridge?" roared the Troll.

"It is only I, Little Billy-goat Gruff, going across the river to make myself fat," said Little Billy-goat Gruff, in such a small voice.

"Now I'm coming to gobble you up," said the Troll.

"Oh please don't eat me, I'm so small," said Little Billy-goat Gruff. "Wait for the next billy-goat, he's much bigger."

"Well, be off with you," said the Troll.

A little while later, Middle Billy-goat Gruff stepped on to the bridge. TRIP TRAP, TRIP TRAP, went his hoofs.

"Who's that tripping over my bridge?" roared the Troll.

"It is only I, Middle Billy-goat Gruff, going across the river to make myself fat," said Middle Billy-goat Gruff, whose voice was not so small.

"Now I'm coming to gobble you up," said the Troll.

"Oh no, don't eat me," said Middle Billy-goat Gruff. "Wait for the next billy-goat, he's the biggest of all."

"Very well, be off with you," said the Troll.

It wasn't long before Big Billy-goat Gruff stepped on to the bridge.

TRIP TRAP, TRIP TRAP, TRIP TRAP, went his hoofs, and the bridge groaned under his weight.

"Who's that tramping over my bridge?" roared the Troll.

"It is I, Big Billy-goat Gruff," said Big Billy-goat Gruff, who had a rough, roaring voice of his own.

"Now I'm coming to gobble you up," said the Troll, and at once he jumped on to the bridge, immensely horrible and hungry.

But Big Billy-goat Gruff was very fierce and strong. He put down his head and charged the Troll and butted him so hard he flew high into the air and then fell down, down, down, *splash* into the middle of the river. And the great ugly Troll was never seen again.

Then Big Billy-goat Gruff joined Middle Billy-goat Gruff and Little Billy-goat Gruff in the field on the far side of the river. There they got so fat that they could hardly walk home again, and if the fat hasn't fallen off them, they're still fat now.

So *snip, snap, snout,* this tale's told out!

John Joe and the Big Hen

by **Martin Waddell**   illustrated by **Paul Howard**

"It's your day for minding John Joe," Mammy told Sammy, so he had to stay with John Joe. Mary read her book and Mammy went on with her work. Splinter the dog sat in the sun and got toasted.

Sammy got bored minding John Joe. Sammy wanted to play with his friend, Willie Brennan. "I'm away down Cow Lane to the Brennans'," Sammy told Mary.

"Take John Joe with you," said Mary, but Sammy took Splinter instead of John Joe.

"I'm left by myself!" John Joe told Mary. "You'd better tell Mammy!"

"Let Mammy get on with her work," Mary said. "I'll settle our Sammy!"

Mary took John Joe by the hand and set off down Cow Lane to find Sammy.

They went to the Brennans', but there was no sign of Sammy! Mary was mad, for it wasn't her day for minding John Joe.

"Do you think they'd be down by the stream?" asked John Joe.

"I'd look, but you are too little to go," Mary said. "And I can't leave you here with no one to mind you."

"I'll mind myself!" said John Joe.

The Brennans' big hen came to look at John Joe. John Joe was used to the hens at his house, but he didn't know the Brennans' big hen.

"I'm not scared of you!" John Joe told the hen.

"I'll whack your backside," John Joe told the hen.

"Go away home, hen!" John Joe told the hen … but the big hen didn't go.

John Joe climbed on the wall, for he thought that the Brennans' big hen might eat him.

"MRS BRENNAN!" shouted John Joe, but Mrs Brennan was out.

"MARY!" yelled John Joe, but Mary had gone after Sammy and she couldn't hear him.

"OH MAMMY!" wailed John Joe, but Mammy was safe back at home.

That left John Joe alone with the Brennans' big hen and so … John Joe ran away from the hen!

Mary came back to the Brennans'
with Sammy and Splinter, but…

"Where's our John Joe?" Sammy
said.

"JOHN JOE! JOHN JOE! OUR JOHN
JOE!" shouted Sammy.

"JOHN JOE!" shouted Mary.

No John Joe with the hens in the yard.
No John Joe with the pigs in the sty.

No John Joe in the ditch.
No John Joe in the barn.

"Go find John Joe, Splinter!" said
Sammy.

Splinter walked round and sniffed at
the ground … and the wall … and the
top of the wall.

Then Splinter dived into the corn.

Splinter barked and he barked and
he barked…

16

WOOF! WOOF! WOOF!

John Joe was asleep in the corn.

"The big hen chased me!" said John Joe.

"We thought you were lost," said Mary, as she carried John Joe up the lane.

"John Joe was scared by the Brennans' big hen," Mary told Mammy. "He hid away in the corn. We thought that we'd lost our little John Joe."

"There's no way I'm losing my little John Joe!" Mammy said.

"It was your day for minding John Joe," Mary told Sammy.

"Sure, I minded myself," said John Joe.

Contrary Mary
by Anita Jeram

When Mary got up this morning she was feeling contrary. She put her cap on back to front and her shoes on the wrong feet.

"Are you awake, Mary?" her mum called.

"No!" said Contrary Mary.

For breakfast there was hot toast with peanut butter.

"What would you like, Mary?" asked Mum.

"Roast potatoes and gravy, please," said Contrary Mary.

When they went to the shops it was raining.

"Come under the umbrella, Mary," said Mum.

But Contrary Mary didn't. She just danced about, getting wet.

All day long, Contrary Mary did contrary things. She rode her bicycle, backwards. She went for a walk, on her hands. She read a book upside down.

She flew her kite along the ground.

Mary's mum shook her head.

"Mary, Mary, quite contrary," she said.

And then she had an idea.

That evening, at bedtime, instead of tucking Mary in the right way round, Mary's mum tucked her in upside down.

Then she opened the curtains, turned on the light, kissed Mary's toes and said, "Good morning!"

Mary laughed and laughed.

"Contrary Mum!" she said.

"Do you love me, Contrary Mary?" asked Mary's mum, giving her a cuddle.

"No!" said Contrary Mary. And she gave her mum a great big kiss.

19

CUDDLY DUDLEY

Dudley loved to play. He loved to play jumping, diving and splashing. But most of all Dudley loved to play . . . all by himself.

The trouble was, Dudley was such a lovely cuddly penguin that whenever his brothers and sisters found him on his own they just couldn't resist having a huddle and a waddle and a cuddle with him.

"Go away," Dudley would say. "Leave me alone."

"We can't," came the reply. "You're just too cuddly, Dudley."

"I'm fed up with all your huddling and waddling and cuddling," said Dudley one day. "I'm going to find a place where I can play all on my own."

And off he went.

He waddled and he toddled for many, many miles until, quite by chance, he found a little wooden house which looked perfect for a penguin.

And it seemed to be empty.

"At last!" said Dudley. "A house of my own – a place where I can jump about all day without being disturbed."

Just then there came a rap-tap-tap at the little wooden door.

"It's us," said two of Dudley's sisters. "We followed your waddleprints. Can we come in?"

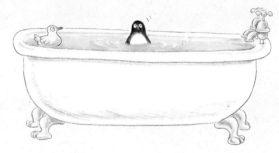

"No, you jolly well can't," said Dudley. "I'm very busy and I don't want to be disturbed, so please go away." And he shut the little wooden door and was alone once more.

"At last!" said Dudley. "A house of my own – a place where I can splash about all day without being..."

Just then there came a rap-tap-tap at the little wooden door.

"It's us," said his brothers and sisters. "We followed your waddleprints. Can we come in and...?"

"No, you jolly well can't," said Dudley. "I don't want

BY JEZ ALBOROUGH

to huddle and waddle and cuddle. So for the very last time ... STOP FOLLOWING ME AROUND!"

He slammed the little wooden door and was alone once more.

"At last!" sighed Dudley. "A house of my own..."

BANG, BANG, BANG went the little wooden door.

"That does it," he said. "When I catch those penguins I'll..."

But it wasn't the penguins at the little wooden door. It was a great big man.

"My word!" said the great big man. "What an adorable penguin! *Give us a cuddle!*" he cried, and chased Dudley all round the house and out into the snow.

Dudley ran and ran and escaped from the man. Then he decided to head back home. But which way was home?

Crunch, crunch, crunch went Dudley, looking for some waddleprints to follow. But when night came, he was still alone ... and completely lost ... and now, for the first time, he was lonely. He climbed a hill to get a better view, and at the top

he saw an enormous orange moon with hundreds of tiny sparkling stars huddled all around.

"Excuse me," said a penguin from the foot of the hill. "Have you finished being alone yet? Only we wondered, now that you're back ... if you wouldn't mind ... whether we could ... it's just that you're so ... *so* ..."

"CUDDLY!" shouted Dudley. And he bounced down the hill as fast as he could.

Then Dudley and all his brothers and sisters had the best huddling, waddling, cuddling session that they'd *ever* had. UNTIL ...

"GIVE US A CUDDLE!"

Quacky quack-quack!

by **Ian Whybrow**   illustrated by **Russell Ayto**

This little baby had some bread;
His mummy gave it to him
  for the ducks,
But he started eating it instead.

Lots of little ducky things
  came swimming along,
Thinking it was feeding time,
  but they were wrong!

The baby held on to the bag,
  he wouldn't let go;
And the crowd of noisy ducky birds
  started to grow.

They made a lot of ducky noises …
  quacky quack-quack!
Then a whole load of geese swam up
  and went *honk! honk!* at the back.

And when a band went marching by,
  in gold and red and black,
Nobody could hear the tune –
  all they could hear was …
  honk! honk! quacky quack-quack!

honk!
honk!

quacky quack-
quack!

toot! toot!

"Louder, boys," said the bandmaster,
  "give it a bit more puff."
So the band went *toot! toot!*
  ever so loud,
But it still wasn't enough.

Then all over the city,
  including the city zoo,
All the animals heard the noise and
  started making noises too.

All the donkeys went *ee-aw! ee-aw!*
All the dogs went *woof! woof!*
All the snakes went *sss-ssss!*
All the crocodiles went *snap! snap!*
All the mice went *squeaky-squeaky!*
All the lions went …

roar!

ee-aw! ee-aw!

woof! woof!

sss-ssss!

snap! snap!

squeaky-squeaky!

Then one little boy piped up and said,
"I know what this is all about.
That's my baby brother with the
  bag of bread;
I'll soon have this sorted out."

He ran over to where the baby
  was holding his bag of bread
And not giving any to the birdies,
  but eating it instead.

And he said, "What about some
  for the ducky birds?"
But the baby started to …

scream!

So his brother said, "If you let me
  hold the bag,
I'll let you hold my ice-cream."

Then the boy said, "Quiet all
  you quack-quacks!
And stop pushing, you're all
  going to get fed."
And he put his hand in the paper bag
  and brought out a handful of bread.

So all the birds went quiet
  and the band stopped playing too…
And all the animals stopped
  making a noise,
Including the animals in the zoo.

And suddenly the baby realized
  they were all waiting for a crumb!
So he gave the ice-cream back
  and he took a great big handful
    of bread and …
Threw all the ducky birds some.

Then all the hungry ducky birds
 were ever so glad they'd come,
And instead of going …
  honk! honk! quacky quack-quack!
All the birdies said …

YUM! YUM!

Marlon sat on the floor watching TV. Marlon's granny sat in the armchair, watching Marlon.

"He's getting too old for that dummy," she said sternly to Marlon's mum.

"It's a noo-noo," said Marlon.

"He calls it a noo-noo," explained Marlon's mum.

"Well, what*ever* he calls it," said Marlon's granny, "he looks like an idiot with that stupid great *thing* stuck in his mouth all the time."

"He doesn't have it *all* the time," soothed Marlon's mum. "Only at night or if he's a bit tired. He's a bit tired now – aren't you, pet?"

"Mmmmm," said Marlon.

"His teeth will start sticking out," warned Marlon's granny.

"Monsters' teeth stick out anyway," observed Marlon.

"Don't answer back," said Marlon's granny. "You should just throw them *all* away," she continued. "At this rate he'll be starting *school* with a dummy. At this rate he'll be starting *work* with a dummy. You'll just have to be firm with him."

"Well," said Marlon's mum, "I am *thinking* about it. We'll start next week, won't we Marlon? Now you're a big boy, we'll just get rid of all those silly noo-noos, won't we?"

"No," said Marlon.

"You see!" said Marlon's granny. "One word from you and he does as he likes."

There was no doubt about it. Marlon was a hopeless case.

Marlon's mum decided to take drastic action. She gathered up every single noo-noo she could find and dumped them all in the dustbin five minutes before the rubbish truck arrived. But Marlon had made plans just in case the worst should happen. He had secret noo-noo supplies all over the house.

NOO-NOO

by Jill Murphy

There was a yellow one down the side of the armchair, a blue one at the back of the breadbin, various different types in his toy ambulance and his favourite pink one was lurking in the toe of his wellington boot.

His mother and granny were astonished. They could not think where he kept finding them.

"You'll be teased when you go out to play," warned his granny. "A great big monster like you with a baby's dummy."

Marlon knew about this already. The other monsters had been teasing him for ages, but he loved his noo-noos so much that he didn't care.

The other monsters often lay in wait and jumped out on Marlon as he passed by with his noo-noo twirling.

"Who's a big baby, then?" jeered Basher.

"Does the little baby need his dummy, then?" sneered Alligatina.

"Who's his mummy's little darling?" cooed Boomps-a-daisy.

Marlon always ignored their taunts.

"You're just jealous," he replied. "You all wish you'd got one too."

Gradually, the secret supply of noo-noos dwindled. Marlon's mum refused to buy any more and they all began to be lost, or thrown away by Marlon's mum. Finally, there was only one left, the pink one. Marlon kept it with him all the time. Either in his mouth or under his pillow or in the toe of his wellington boot, where no one thought to look.

To his delight, Marlon found one extra noo-noo that his mum had missed. It was a blue one, which had fallen down the side of his bed and been covered up by a sock. He knew his best pink noo-noo wouldn't last for ever, so he crept out and planted the blue one in the garden.

All the other monsters decided to gang up on Marlon. They collected lots of different bits of junk and fixed them all together until they had made just what they wanted. It was a noo-noo snatcher.

Then they waited behind a bush until Marlon came past with his pink noo-noo twirling.

"Here he comes," said Alligatina.

"Grab it!" yelled Boomps-a-daisy.

"Now!" said Basher.

With one quick hooking movement, they caught the ring of the noo-noo with the noo-noo snatcher and pulled!

But Marlon clenched his teeth and held on. Monsters have the most powerful jaws in the world. Once they have decided to hang on, that's *it*. Marlon hung on, the monsters hung on to the noo-noo snatcher and there they stayed, both sides pulling with all their monster might.

And there they would *still* be, if Marlon had not decided, just at that very moment, that perhaps he was too old to have a noo-noo any more.

So, he let go. And all the other monsters went whizzing off down the road, across the park and into the pond with a mighty splash.

Marlon went home. "I've given up my noo-noo," he said. "I sort of threw it into the pond."

"Good gracious me!" exclaimed Marlon's mum, sitting down suddenly with the shock.

"I told you," said Marlon's granny. "You just have to be firm."

"Actually," said Marlon, "I've planted one, so I'll have a noo-noo tree – just in case I change my mind."

"That's nice, dear," said Marlon's mum.

"Nonsense!" said Marlon's granny. "Dummies don't grow on trees. A noo-noo tree! How ridiculous!"

Two Shoes, New Shoes

Two shoes, new shoes,
  Bright shiny blue shoes.

High-heeled ladies' shoes
  For standing tall,
Button-up baby's shoes,
  Soft and small.

Slippers, warm by the fire,
  Lace-ups in the street.
Gloves are for hands
  And socks are for feet.

A crown made of paper,
  A hat with a feather,
Sun hats, fun hats,
  Hats for bad weather.

by Shirley Hughes

A clean white T-shirt
  Laid on the bed,
Two holes for arms
  And one for the head.

Zip up a zipper,
  Button a coat,
A shoe for a bed,
  A hat for a boat.

Wearing it short
  And wearing it long,
Getting it right
  And getting it wrong.

Trailing finery,
  Dressed for a ball
And into the bath
  Wearing nothing at all!

THIS IS THE BEAR
— AND THE —
BAD LITTLE GIRL

by Sarah Hayes   *illustrated by* Helen Craig

This is the bear who went out to eat.
This is the dog who stayed in the street.

This is the girl with the curly hair
who said she really liked the bear.

This is the dog who put out a paw
and tripped the woman who came in the door …

which pushed the people waiting to pay
and made the waiter drop the tray.

This is the boy all covered in cream
who went to the kitchen to wash his face clean.

This is the girl with the curly hair
who said, "You're coming with me, bear."

This is the girl who walked down the street
holding the bear by one of his feet.

This is the dog who thought it was fun
when the bad little girl began to run.

This is the girl who ran faster and faster
but this is the dog who ran right past her.

This is the girl
who gave the bear back
and said he was
only a baggy old sack.
This is the boy
who said, "I don't care
if he's saggy or baggy,
he's still *my* bear."

My Mum and Dad Make Me Laugh

My mum and dad make me laugh. One likes spots and the other likes stripes.

My mum likes spots in winter and spots in summer. My dad likes stripes on weekdays and stripes at weekends.

by Nick Sharratt

Last weekend we went to the safari park. My mum put on her spottiest dress and earrings, and my dad put on his stripiest suit and tie.
I put on my grey top and trousers.
"You do like funny clothes!" said my mum and dad.

We set off in the car and on the way we stopped for something to eat.
My mum had a spotty pizza and my dad had a stripy ice-cream.
I had a bun.
"You do like funny food!" said my mum and dad.

When we got to the safari park it was very exciting.
My mum liked the big cats best.
"Those are splendid spots," she said. "And I should know!"
My dad liked the zebras best.
"Those are super stripes," he said. "And I should know!"

But the animals I liked best didn't have spots and didn't have stripes.
They were big and grey and eating their tea.
"Those are really good elephants," I said.

"And I should know!"

Gran and Grandpa

by Helen Oxenbury

I love visiting
Gran and Grandpa.
I go every week.
"Tell us what you've been
doing all week," they say.
I tell them everything.

Then sometimes I teach
them a new song I learned
at school. But they
never get the tune
quite right.

"Come on, Gran! Let's go and
look at all your things," I say.
Gran has such interesting
drawers and boxes.

"How are your
tomatoes, Grandpa?"
"I've saved you the first ripe
one to pick," he says.

"I'll get the lunch now," says Gran.
"Come and make a house
with me, Grandpa,"
I say.

"Lunch is ready!" calls Gran. Grandpa can't get up. "You shouldn't play these games at your age," Gran tells him.

"We could play hospitals now," I say after lunch. Gran and Grandpa let me do anything to them.

"I'll just get more bandages," I say. When I get back they're both asleep. So I watch television quietly until Dad comes.

MOUSE PARTY

Mouse found a deserted house and decided to make his home there.

But it was a very big house for such a small mouse and he felt a little lonely.

"I know," he thought, "I'll have a party." So he sent invitations to all his friends.

The first to arrive were…

Cat with a **mat**   and **Dog** with a **log.**

Then came **Hare** with a **chair,**   **Owl** with a **towel,**

Giraffe with a **bath,**   **Hen** with a **pen,**

Lamb with some **jam,**   **Rat** with a **bat** in a **hat**

and **Fox** with a **box** full of **lots** and **lots** of different kinds and colours of **socks.**

"Let's party!" said Mouse. But…

Rat-a-tat-tat!

It was an elephant with two trunks. He was

blowing through one and carrying the other.

"Hello," said Mouse. "Welcome to my house."

"*Your* house?" said the elephant and he looked rather cross.

"I've just been away on a long holiday.

This house, I must tell you, is mine!"

42

by **Alan Durant**
illustrated by **Sue Heap**

"Oh," said Mouse, Lamb, Hare, Rat and Bat.

"Oh," said Hen, Dog, Owl, Fox and Giraffe.

But, "Come in, come in!" said Cat. "You're just in time for the party."

"A party … for me?" said Elephant. "Oh my! Yippee!"

So they drank and they ate and they danced until late and had the most

marvellous party. And later, when the guests had all gone home,

leaving Elephant and Mouse alone,

Elephant said, "I think, little Mouse, perhaps it's true,

there's room for us both in this house, don't you?"

43

BEARS IN THE FOREST

by Karen Wallace illustrated by Barbara Firth

Deep in a cave, a mother bear sleeps. She is huge and warm. Her heart beats slowly. Outside it is cold and the trees are covered in snow. Her newborn cubs are blind and tiny. They find her milk and begin to grow.

Snow slips from the trees and melts on the ground. The ice has broken on the lake. Mother bear wakes. Her long sleep is over. She leads her cubs down to the lake shore. She slurps and slurps the freezing water.

Leaves burst from their buds. There are frogs' eggs in the lake. Mother bear snuffs the air for strange smells, listens for strange sounds. Her cubs know nothing of the forest. This is their first spring. Mother bear must take care.

The summer sun is hot. Mother bear sits in a tree stump. Angry bees buzz around her head, and stolen honey drops from her paws.

Her two skinny bear cubs wrestle in the long grass. They squeal like little boys and roll over and over away from their mother. Mother bear growls.

Come back! There are dangers in the forest! Her cubs do not hear her. Mother bear snorts. She is angry. She strides across the meadow and whacks them with a heavy paw.

Two frightened bear cubs scramble up the nearest tree. Mother bear waits below, still as a statue, listening to the forest. When she feels safe, she will call her cubs down. Mother bear must take care.

Soon the days grow shorter and squirrels start to hide acorns. Bushes are bright with berries. Seed pods flutter to the ground. Winter is coming. Mother bear and her cubs eat everything they can find.

Icy winds blast the forest. Mother bear plods through the snow. Her cubs are fat. Their fur is thick. She chooses a shelter that is dark and dry, where they will sleep through the long winter months. When spring has woken the bears again, mother bear leads her cubs to

the river. She follows a trail worn deep in the ground. Hundreds of bears have walked this way before her. The river runs deep and fast. Mother bear wades in. Soon a silver trout flashes in her jaws. The cubs are hungry. They wade into the river and catch their own fish.

Mother bear gobbles berries. Her cubs are playing where she can't see them. They are almost grown. Soon they will leave her. Mother bear has taught them everything she knows.

The Red Woollen Blanket

by *Bob Graham*

Julia had her own blanket right from the start. Julia was born in the winter. She slept in her special cot wrapped tight as a parcel. She had a band of plastic on her wrist with her name on it.

"She's as bald as an egg," said her father, helping himself to another chocolate.

Julia came home from the hospital with her new red blanket, a bear, a grey woollen dog and a plastic duck.

Waiting at home for her were a large pair of pants with pink flowers and a beautiful blue jacket specially knitted by her grandmother.

"Isn't blue for boys?" said Dad.

"No, it doesn't really matter," said Mum.

Wrapped up in the red woollen blanket, Julia slept in her own basket or in the front garden in the watery winter sunshine. Her hair sprouted from the holes in her tea-cosy hat. She smiled – nothing worried Julia.

Julia grew. She slept in a cot and sucked and chewed the corners of her not-so-new blanket. She rubbed the red woollen blanket gently against her nose.

Julia's mum carried her to the shops in a pack on her back. The pack was meant to carry the shopping. Julia liked it so much up there that the pushchair was used for the shopping and the pack was used for Julia.

Then Julia was crawling and her blanket went with her. Some of it was left behind…

Then Julia took her first step.

Julia made her own small room from the blanket. It was pink twilight under there. From outside, the "creature" had a mind of its own.
It heaved and throbbed.

Wherever Julia went her blanket went too. In the spring, the summer, the autumn, and the winter.

Julia was getting bigger. Her blanket was getting smaller.

A sizeable piece was lost under the lawnmower.

"If Julia ran off deep into a forest," said her father, "she could find her way back by the blanket threads left behind."

The day that Julia started school, she had a handy little blanket not much bigger than a postage stamp – because it would never do to take a whole blanket to school … unless you were Billy, who used his blanket as a "Lone Avenger's" cape.

Sometime during Julia's first day at school, she lost the last threads of her blanket.

It may have been while playing in the school yard, or having her lunch under the trees. It could have been anywhere at all …

and she hardly missed it.

HANDA'S SURPRISE

Handa put seven delicious fruits in a basket
for her friend, Akeyo.
She will be surprised, thought Handa
as she set off for Akeyo's village.
I wonder which fruit she'll like best?

Will she like
the soft yellow banana …

or the sweet-
smelling guava?

Will she like the
round juicy orange …

by Eileen Browne

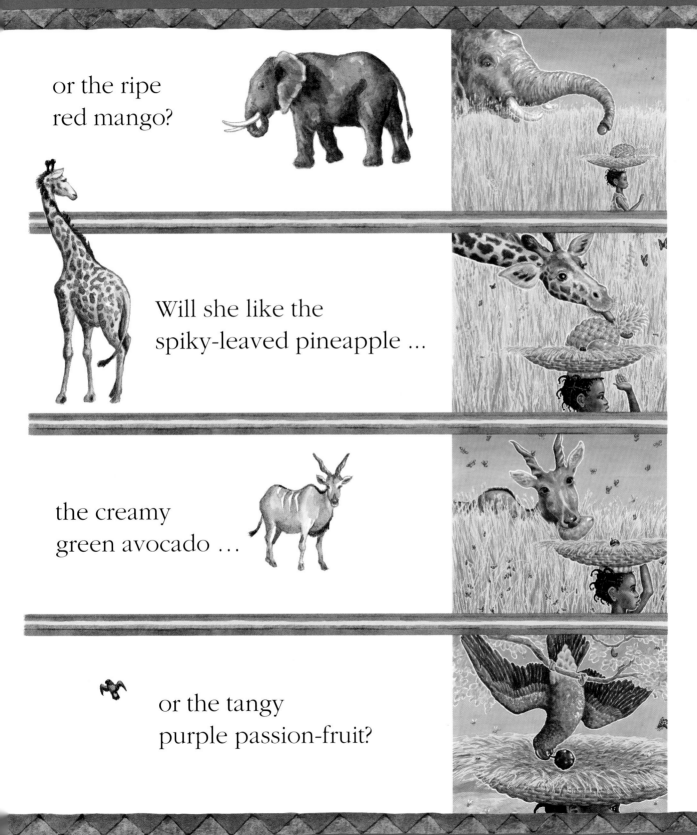

or the ripe
red mango?

Will she like the
spiky-leaved pineapple ...

the creamy
green avocado ...

or the tangy
purple passion-fruit?

Which fruit will Akeyo like best?

"Hello, Akeyo," said Handa. "I've brought you a surprise."
"Tangerines!" said Akeyo. "My favourite fruit."

"TANGERINES?" said Handa. "That *is* a surprise!"

SEBASTIAN'S TRUMPET

by Miko Imai

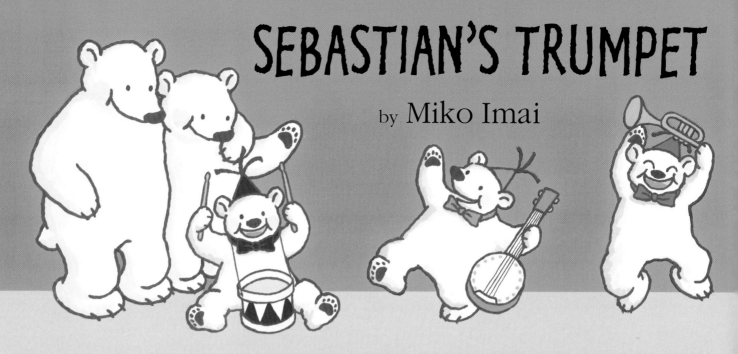

It was the three little bears' birthday. Daddy and Mummy Bear had some special presents for them. Theodore got a drum. Oswald got a banjo. And Sebastian got a trumpet.

"Let's play 'Happy Birthday!'" they shouted.
Theodore banged on his drum. Rat-a-tat-tat.
Oswald strummed his banjo. Twang Twang.
And Sebastian blew into his trumpet.
But the only sound it made was Pfffft.

"What's happened to your trumpet?" asked Theodore. "Let *me* try it … Pfffftt."
"Let *me* try!" said Oswald. "I bet I can do it … Pffffftt."

Theodore and Oswald played "Happy Birthday" for Daddy and Mummy Bear.

I wish I could play my trumpet, thought Sebastian.

"Pffftt … I HATE this trumpet!" Sebastian sobbed.

54

"Why did you give me a trumpet, Mummy?
It doesn't even work!"
"Maybe you're trying too hard," said Mummy
Bear. "Why don't you rest now and try
again later?"

When Sebastian woke up, he couldn't
wait to try his trumpet again.
He tiptoed towards it.

He picked it up and started to play.

Pffooott

Troooft

TA-TA-TA-
ROOOOOOON!
TA-TA-TA-
ROOOOOOON!

"You did it, Sebastian!" his brothers shouted.
And the three little bears all played
"Happy Birthday" together.

Twang
Twang

Rat-a-tat-tat

Toot
Toot

WHERE'S MY MUM?

by Leon Rosselson

illustrated by Priscilla Lamont

Where's my mum?
She's not in the drawer,
Or under the bed,
Or behind the door.

She's not in the bath,
Unless she's got
Turned into
  a spider.
I hope she's not!

I'll look in the mirror;
Who can that be
With the scowly face?
It must be me!

She's not in the fridge
With the strawberry jelly,
The chicken, the milk and
The something smelly.

She's not in the cupboard.
What's that noise?
No, she's not
  in the box
With all my
  toys.

She's not
  in the piano
Or under the chair,
Or behind the curtains
Or anywhere.

I'll try the garden.
Where can she be?
She's not in the sky
Or the apple tree.

Look at those ants
  racing to
  and fro!
Have you seen
  my mum?
I think that
  means no.

I can't see a mum
In the garden shed,
And she isn't a flower
In the flowerbed!

Perhaps she's in *her* bed.
I'll go and explore.
Back into the house;
Push open her door.

There's a lumpy shape –
I'll take a peep…
There's my mum,
And she's fast asleep!

Mum! Mum!
You should be awake.
Tell me a story!
Bake me a cake!

Mum! I can hop!
I can jump on the bed!
I can curl in a ball,
I can stand on my head.

Paint me a picture.
Play games
    with me.
Mum! I'm hungry.
I want my tea.

Can I drink my milk in
My dinosaur mug?
Get up, Mum…
    And I'll give you a hug!

MONKEY TRICKS

Horatio was practising hopping. HOP HOP HOP WHOOPS! He fell over a notice board. I'll ask James what this says, he thought.

James was looking in his Useful Box. Someone had untidied it. "What does this say?" asked Horatio.

"Johnny Conqueror Coming Today," said James. He looked worried.

"That naughty monkey!" Horatio looked all around for Johnny Conqueror.

by Camilla Ashforth

"Jimmies and Jacks! Mind your backs!" a voice called, and there was Johnny Conqueror, pulling a wagon.

"I'm very good at juggling," he boasted.

He threw a string of beads into the air and held out his hands to catch them. But he missed and the beads scattered everywhere. Horatio clapped his hands.

My beads look like this, thought James, picking one up.

"For my next trick," shouted Johnny Conqueror, "I take a long piece of rope and knot it here and twist it a bit here…"

That rope looks useful, thought James.

He looked in his Useful Box again.

Johnny Conqueror got into a tangle. He needed James to untie him. Horatio thought it was very funny.

"I'll show you how clever I am at balancing," said Johnny Conqueror, jumping onto a cotton reel! He stood on one leg and spun a dish above him. The cotton reel wobbled.

James looked worried. If that was my dish … he thought.

CRASH! The cotton reel spun away. Johnny Conqueror fell over. The dish broke. Oh dear, thought James.

"Hooray!" shouted Horatio.

"To end the show," announced Johnny Conqueror, "I do my best trick. I disappear! All close your eyes and count to five."

"One … two …" Horatio began.

"I know who untidied my Useful Box," whispered James.

"Three … four …" added Horatio.

"And I'm going to catch him," James said.

"Five!" shouted Horatio and they opened their eyes. Johnny Conqueror had disappeared.

"Bother," said James. "He got away."

James began to tidy up.

"Now I can show you my trick," said Horatio, and he hopped for James. James clapped his hands.

"That really is clever," he said, and gave Horatio a big hug.

OOPS-A-DAISY!
by Joyce Dunbar   illustrated by Carol Thompson

Sadie came to play.
"I can be upside down," said Sadie.
"So can I," I said.
"I can go head over heels," said Sadie.

"So can I," I said.

"I can wear my trousers inside out,"
  said Sadie.
"So can I," I said.

"I can put my jumper back to front,"
  said Sadie.
"So can I," I said.

"Let's be back to
  back," said Sadie.
And we were.

"Let's be higgledy-piggledy,"
 said Sadie.
 And we were.

"Let's go oops-a-daisy," said Sadie. And we did.
 Sadie bumped her head on mine.
 I bumped my head on Sadie's.

"Ooow!" Sadie yowled.

"Ouch!" I howled.

"That was good fun, wasn't it?" said Sadie.
 "Let's play it again," I said.

MISS POLLY

Miss Polly
had a dolly
Who was sick, sick, sick,

So she phoned
for the doctor
To be quick, quick, quick.

The doctor came
With his bag and his hat,

And he rapped at the door
With a rat-tat-tat.

illustrated by **Toni Goffe**

He looked
at the dolly
And he shook his head.

Then he said,
"Miss Polly,
Put her straight to bed."

He wrote on a paper
For a pill, pill, pill.

"I'll be back in the morning
With my bill, bill, bill."

65

The Little Boat

by Kathy Henderson

illustrated by Patrick Benson

Down by the shore
where the sea meets the land,
licking at the pebbles
sucking at the sand,
and the wind flaps
the sunshades
and the ice-cream man
out-shouts the seagulls
and the people come
with buckets and spades
and suntan lotion
to play on the shore
by the edge of the ocean,

a little boy
made himself a boat
from an old piece of
polystyrene plastic,
with a stick for a mast
and a string tail sail
and he splashed
and he played
with the boat he'd made
digging it a harbour
scooping it a creek,
all day long by the edge
of the sea,
singing
*'We are unsinkable
my boat and me!'*

Until he turned his back
and a small wind blew
and the little boat drifted
away from the shore,
out of his reach
across the waves,
past the swimmers
and air beds,
away from the beach.

And the boat
sailed out
in the skim of the wind
past the fishermen
sitting on the end of the pier,

out and out
past a crab boat trailing
a row of floats
and a dinghy sailing
a zig-zag track
across the wind,

out where the lighthouse
beam beats by
where the sea birds wheel
in the sky and dive
for the silvery fish
just beneath the waves,
out sailed the little boat
out and away.

And it bobbed by
a tugboat chugging home
from leading a liner
out to sea
and it churned in the wake,
still further out,
of a giant tanker
as high as a house
and as long as a road,
on sailed the little boat
all alone.

And the further it sailed
the bigger grew
the ocean

until all around
was sea
and not a sign of land,
not a leaf,
not a bird,
not a sound,
just the wind
and heaving sliding
gliding breathing water
under endless sky.

And hours went by
and days went by
and still the little boat
sailed on,
with once a glimpse
of the lights from an oil rig
standing in the distance
on giant's legs
and sometimes
the shape of a ship
like a toy,
hanging in the air
at the rim of the world,

or a bit of driftwood
or rubbish passing,
otherwise nothing,
on and on.

And then came a day
when the sky went dark
and the seas grew uneasy
and tossed about
and the wind
that had whispered
began to roar
and the waves grew bigger
and lashed and tore
and hurled great manes
of spray
in the air
like flames in a fire

and all night long
as the seas grew rougher
the little boat danced
with the wind
and the weather

till the morning came
and the storm was over
and all was calm and still
and quiet again.

68

And then suddenly
up from underneath
with a thrust and a leap
and a mouth full of teeth
came a great fish snapping
for something to eat,
and it grabbed the boat
and dived
deep
deep
deep
down
to where the light grows dim
in the depths of the sea,
a world of fins and claws
and slippery things
and rocks and wrecks
of ancient ships
and ocean creatures
no one's seen

where,
finding that plastic
wasn't food,
the fish spat out
the boat again
and up it flew,
up up up up
like the flight of an arrow
towards the light,
burst through the silver skin
of the sea
and floated on
in the calm sunshine.

Then a small breeze came
and the small breeze grew,
steadily pushing
the boat along,
and now sea birds called
in the sky again
and a boat sailed near
and another
and then,
in the beat of the sun
and the silent air,
a sound could be heard,
waves breaking somewhere
and the sea swell curled
and the white surf rolled
the little boat on
and on
towards land.

And there at the shore
where the sea greets the land,
licking at the pebbles
sucking at the sand,
a child was standing,
she stretched out her hand
and picked up the boat
from the waves at her feet
and all day long
she splashed and she played
with the boat she'd found
at the edge of the sea,
singing
*'We are unsinkable
my boat and me!'*

"Not me," said the monkey

"Who keeps dropping
banana skins round here?"
growled the lion.
"Not me," said the monkey.

"Who keeps walking
  all over me?"
hissed the snake.
"Not me," growled the lion.
"And not me," said the monkey.

"Who keeps throwing coconuts
  about?" snorted the rhino.
"Not me," hissed the snake.
"Not me," growled the lion.
"And not me," said
  the monkey.

70

by Colin West

"WHO KEEPS TICKLING ME?"
 roared the elephant.
"Not me," snorted the rhino.
"Not me," hissed the snake.
"Not me," growled the lion.
"And not ME!" said the monkey.

Slurp! Slurp! Slurp! went the elephant.

WHOOOOSH!

"Now who's going to stop all this monkey business?"
laughed the lion, and the snake,
and the rhino,
and the elephant.

"Well…
NOT ME!" said You-Know-Who.

The Fat King

Once upon a time there was a fat king.

He lived in a fat house with his fat wife and fat children. He had a fat dog and a fat cat. And fat birds sat in fat trees under a fat sun. Everything in the garden was fat.

One day the king came downstairs and said hello to his kingdom. "Hello, dog and cat," he said.

"Hello, cabbages. Hello, potatoes. Hello, trees. Hello, world."

But when he came to the green oak tree he stopped and stared.

"Come and see this," he called to his wife and children. For there, under the tree, sitting in its shade, was a THIN bird.

"Shoo!" said the king and clapped his hands. "Shoo, little thin bird!" he said very loudly indeed.

But the little thin bird did not move. So the king gave him a dish of breadcrumbs and went off to consult the gardener.

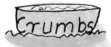

"You could try chasing him," said William.

But the king said, "That will only frighten him. I will go and ask Fido instead."

And on the way to Fido he passed the green oak tree, and put down another dish of crumbs for the little thin bird.

"Hello, Fido," said the king. "I have called about the little thin bird."

by Graham Jeffery

Fido said, "I will come and bark at him." But the king said, "No, I do not want to startle him, I will go and see Tibby instead."

And as he passed the green oak tree he left a dish of milk for the little thin bird.

Tibby said, "I could jump over him and scratch him."

But the king said, "No, that will not do at all. I will go and ask the family. They will think of something kinder."

But his family did not know what to do. And the fisherman didn't know. And the vicar didn't know. And the postman didn't know.

And every time the king passed the green oak tree, he left a bowl of crumbs for the little thin bird.

The fat king said to his friends, "It is no good. It is no good at all. Nobody knows what to do about the little thin bird."

But then Fido looked under the green oak tree, and Tibby looked, and the king looked, and everybody looked.

And there under the green oak tree was … the fattest, plumpest bird you ever saw. And he hopped up into the green oak tree and went to sleep under the fat sun.

73

THE ELEPHANT TREE
by Penny Dale

Elephant wanted to climb a tree. So we went to find the elephant tree.

We walked and we walked. We looked and we looked.

"Is this the elephant tree?" "No," said the birds. "It's the bird tree."

"Is this the elephant tree?" "No," said the monkeys. "It's the monkey tree."

"Is this the elephant tree?"

"No," said the tigers.

"It's the tiger tree."

"Are any of these the elephant tree?"

"No," said the bears. "These are bear trees."

We ran and we ran.

We walked and we walked.

We looked and we looked.

But we still couldn't find the elephant tree.

Never mind, Elephant. Wait and see.

Here it is. Look. The elephant tree.

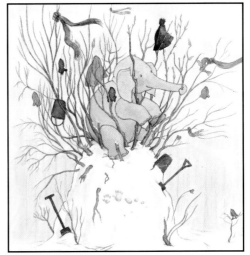

75

MY FRIEND HARRY

The day James bought Harry, Harry's life changed. James talked all the way home. Harry didn't say a thing. He just sat in the car, looking clean and new and neat.

"What are you thinking?" James asked. But Harry never said.

At the beginning of every day, when James woke up, he tossed and rumpled the blankets until Harry fell out of bed.

"Good morning, my friend Harry!" James said. "What shall we do today?" But Harry never said.

BY KIM LEWIS

So in the mornings, James and Harry went everywhere. They climbed to the top of the hill and back again, and travelled from one end of the farm to the other.

In the sun and the wind and the rain, Harry's skin soon began to wrinkle. Once he fell off James' bicycle and James had to mend his head.

In the afternoons James and Harry helped his father and mother – gathering sheep, feeding cattle, fixing tractors and bringing in the hay.

Both James and Harry got very dirty. After many bathtimes Harry's jacket shrank and his skin began to fade.

"What are you thinking?" James asked Harry.

But Harry never said, so James hugged him tight until Harry's ears began to flop and his trunk began to sag.

Sometimes James made Harry stand on his head. Harry never complained.

"My friend Harry!" James always said.

At the end of every day James tucked Harry into bed beside him. He read story after story and talked and talked.

"Are you listening?" he yawned.

But Harry lay close to James and never said, until James' dad came in to kiss them.

James even took Harry on holiday, squeezing him into the dark in a bag with the apple juice. But the juice spilled and made Harry very sticky. James scrubbed Harry and hung him out to dry. Harry swung in the sea breeze, while James and his mum and dad ran in and out of the waves.

Then one day Harry could no longer sit up straight. James propped him up in a chair.

"I'm going to school today!" James said. "What do you think?"

Harry was quiet. James got dressed in brand new clothes, and went a little quiet too.

Harry stayed cuddled up in James' mother's arms while the children played all around in the school yard. When James went into school, his mother waved, then drove home, very quietly, with Harry.

James' mother tucked Harry into James' bed and softly closed the door. Harry lay very still. Cows mooed faintly in the distance. James' father drove the tractor out of the yard. Birds pecked and peeped in the bushes by the house. The sun rose up and went round, warming Harry where he lay, until it was afternoon.

Harry lay still, waiting all by himself, without James.

That night, James told Harry about his day. "I expect I'll go to school again tomorrow," he said.

Harry was very quiet.

James stared into the dark for a long time. "Did you miss me, my friend Harry?" he asked.

The next day, James took Harry to school. "Just this once," he said. "Until you get used to being on your own."

Harry sat very close to James and never said a word.

"My friend Harry," said James.

DOCTOR ELSIE

Doctor Elsie gets up early and has breakfast with her family.

She waves goodbye to Little Elsie and bicycles off to work.

Doctor Elsie puts on her white coat and checks her medicine cupboard.

"Yes, all there," says Doctor Elsie.

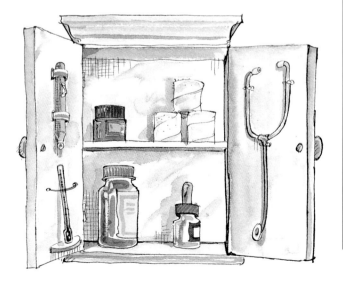

Francis has got a cough. Doctor Elsie listens to his chest.

"Brrr! That's cold!" says Francis.

"I think you need some medicine," says Doctor Elsie.

"Mind you finish it all up!"

Sammy and his twin sister have both got tummy pains.

"Ow! Ooooh! Ow!" they moan.

"Nothing wrong here," says Doctor Elsie. "But there's chocolate all over your faces! Try apples instead."

written by Vivian French
conceived and illustrated by Rowan Barnes-Murphy

There are lots of babies in the baby clinic. Doctor Elsie weighs Hetty's little brother.

"Can I weigh my teddy?" asks Hetty.

Lily's mother rings up. "Lily's fallen down the stairs," she says.

"I'm on my way," says Doctor Elsie.

"Let's see," says Doctor Elsie. "A bump and a graze! Not too bad though. You'll be better in a couple of days."

Then Doctor Elsie hurries away to see Oscar. Oscar has terrible earache.

"Poor old thing," says Doctor Elsie, looking in his ear. "I'll give you a prescription for some ear-drops."

Doctor Elsie is very tired. She bicycles home slowly.

"Don't worry, Mummy," says Little Elsie, "I'll make you better with a kiss."

PROWLPUSS

by Gina Wilson
illustrated by David Parkins

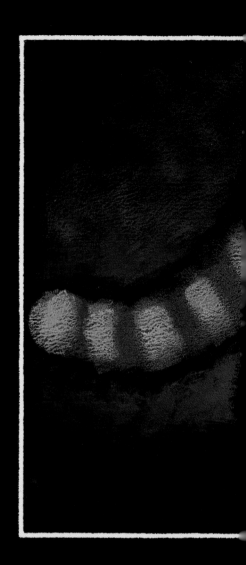

Prowlpuss is cunning
   and wily and sly,
A kingsize cat with
   one ear and one eye.
He's not a
   sit-by-the-fire-
   and-purr cat,
A look-at-my-
   exquisite-fur cat,
No, he's not!

He's rough and gruff
   and very very tough.
Where ya goin',
   Prowlpuss?
AHA!

Down in the alley
   something stirs!
Is it a burglar?
Is it a witch?

Is it a ghoul with
   a bag of bones?
No, it's not!
It's Prowlpuss!

He's not a lap cat,
   a cuddle-up-
   for-a-chat cat,
No, he's not!

He's not a sit-in-
   the-window-
   and-stare cat.
He's an I-WAS-
   THERE! cat.

Watch out!
Prowlpuss about!

He's not a stay-
   at-home cat,
No, he's not!

He's not a sit-on-
   the-mat-and-lick-
   yourself-down cat.
He's an out-on-
   the-town cat,
A racer, a chaser,
A"You're a disgrace"-er!
A "Don't show
   your face"-er!

He's not a throat-
    soft-as-silk cat,
A saucer-of-
    milk cat,
No, he's not!
He's a fat cat,
A rat cat,
A "What on earth
    was that?" cat

So what's it all for –
All the razzle and dazzle,
The crash, bang, wallop,
The yowling,
    the howling,
The "Give us a break!"
"Don't keep us awake!"
"Hoppit!" "Clear off!"
"Get lost!" "Scram!"

"Good riddance!"
    "Go to the devil!"?

Who is
    he wooing
With his
    hullabalooing
Night after night?

AHA!

Back through
  the alley
  slinks Prowlpuss
  at dawn,
Love-lost and lorn.

And old
  Nellie Smith
  in her deep
  feather bed
Lifts her head.

"That's Prowly
  come home!
That's my
  jowly Prowly!
My sweet
  Prowly-wowly!
My sleep-all-
  the-day cat,
My let-the-mice-
  play cat,
My what-did-
  you-say? cat,
My soft and dozy,
Oh-so-cosy,
Tickle-my-toes-y,
Stroke-my-nose-y

PROWLPUSS."

High in a tree
  at the alley's end,
Right at the top
  so no one
  can get her
Or fret her
  or pet her,
Lives one little cat –
A tiny-white-star cat,
A twinkle-afar cat.

In the moonlight
  she dances,
Like snowflakes
  on branches,
She spins
  and she whirls.

But not for long!
In a flash
  she's gone!

Now Prowlpuss
  will sing for her –
What he would
  bring for her!
Oh, how he
  longs for her!
Love of his life!

If she'd *only*
  come down...

But she won't!
  No, she won't!

CLOWN

Peekaboo, how do
you do?

Quick, slow,
catch and throw.

Clip, clop,
jump on top.

Careful, clown,
don't look down!

by **Paul Manning**   *illustrated by* **Nicola Bayley**

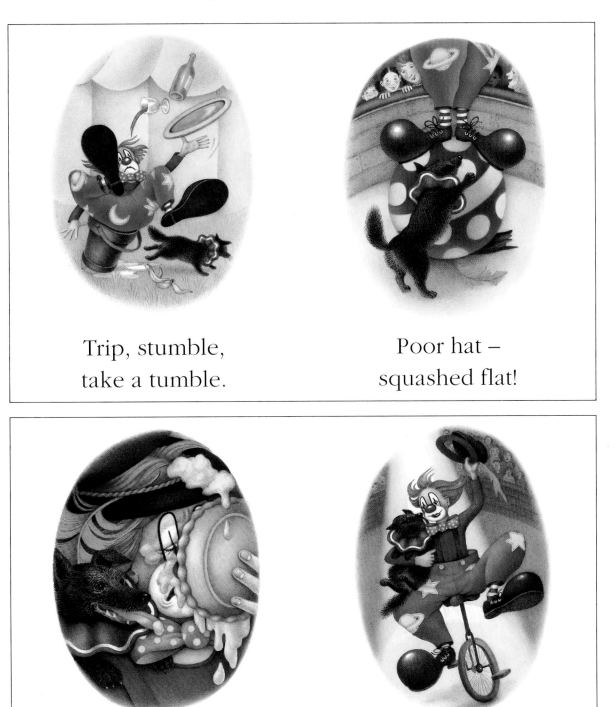

Trip, stumble,
take a tumble.

Poor hat –
squashed flat!

I spy …
a custard pie!

Take a bow,
that's all for now.

SQUEAK-A-LOT

In an old old house lived a small small mouse
   who had no one to play with.
So the small small mouse went out of the house
   to find a friend to play with.

And he found **a bee**.
"Can I play with you?"
the mouse asked the bee.
"Of course," said the bee.
"What will we play?" asked the mouse.
"We'll play Buzz-a-lot," said the bee.

Buzz buzz buzz buzz!

But the mouse didn't like it a lot.
So he went to find a better friend to play with.

And he found **a dog**.
"Can I play with you?" the mouse asked the dog.
"Of course," said the dog.
"What will we play?" asked the mouse.
"We'll play Woof-a-lot," said the dog.

Woof woof woof woof!

But the mouse didn't like it a lot.
So he went to find a better friend to play with.

by **Martin Waddell**
illustrated by **Virginia Miller**

And he found **a chicken**.

"Can I play with you?" the mouse asked the chicken.
"Of course," said the chicken.
"What will we play?" asked the mouse.
"We'll play Cluck-a-lot," said the chicken.

Cluck cluck cluck cluck!

But the mouse didn't like it a lot.
So he went to find a better friend to play with.

And he found **a cat**.
"Can I play with you?"
the mouse asked
the cat. And …

WHAM!

BAM!

SCRAM!

The mouse didn't like
it a lot. So he ran away
through the long long grass
playing Squeak-a-lot all by himself.

Squeak squeak squeak squeak!

Squeak! Some mice found the mouse.
"Can we play with you?" the mice asked the mouse.
"Of course," said the mouse.
"What will we play?" asked the mice.

"Buzz-a-lot!" said the mouse.

Buzz buzz buzz buzz!

And all of them liked it a lot.

"Woof-a-lot!" said the mouse.

Woof woof woof woof!

And all of them liked it a lot.

"Cluck-a-lot!" said the mouse.

Cluck cluck cluck cluck!

And all of them liked it a lot.

"**WHAM! BAM! SCRAM!**" said the mouse.

The mouse chased the mice through the long long grass back home to the old old house. And together they played ...

Sleep-a-lot.

The Big Big Sea

by **Martin Waddell**

illustrated by **Jennifer Eachus**

Mum said, "Let's go!"
So we went
out of the house
and into the dark
and I saw…
THE MOON.

We went over the field
and under the fence
and I saw
the sea in the moonlight,
waiting for me.
Mum said,
"Take off your shoes
and socks!"
And I did.

And I ran
and Mum ran.
We ran and we ran
straight through
the puddles
and out to the sea!

I went right in
to the shiny bit.
There was only me
in the big big sea.

I splashed
and I laughed
and Mum came after me
and we paddled
out deep in the water.

We got all wet.

Then we walked
a bit more
by the edge of the sea
and our feet
made big holes
in the sand.

Far far away
right round the bay
were the town
and the lights
and the mountains.
We felt very small,
Mum and me.

We didn't go to the town.
We just stayed for a while
by the sea.

And Mum said to me,
"Remember this time.
It's the way life should be."

I got cold
and Mum carried me
all the way back.

We sat by the fire,
Mum and me,
and ate hot buttered toast
and I went to sleep
on her knee.

I'll always remember
just Mum and me
and the night
that we walked
by the big big sea.

The Walker Treasury
of First Stories

*Some more collections of stories and poems
for young children*

ISBN 0-7445-6956-7 (pb)

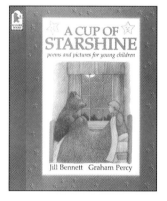

ISBN 0-7445-6097-7 (pb)

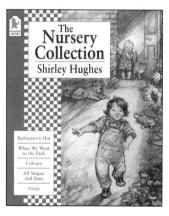

ISBN 0-7445-4378-9 (pb)

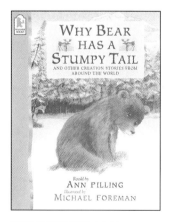

ISBN 0-7445-7289-4 (pb)

ISBN 0-7445-6140-X (hb)

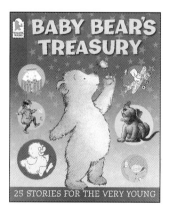

ISBN 0-7445-6957-5 (pb)